The Passover Mouse

by Joy Nelkin Wieder

illustrated by Shahar Kober

Doubleday Books for Young Readers

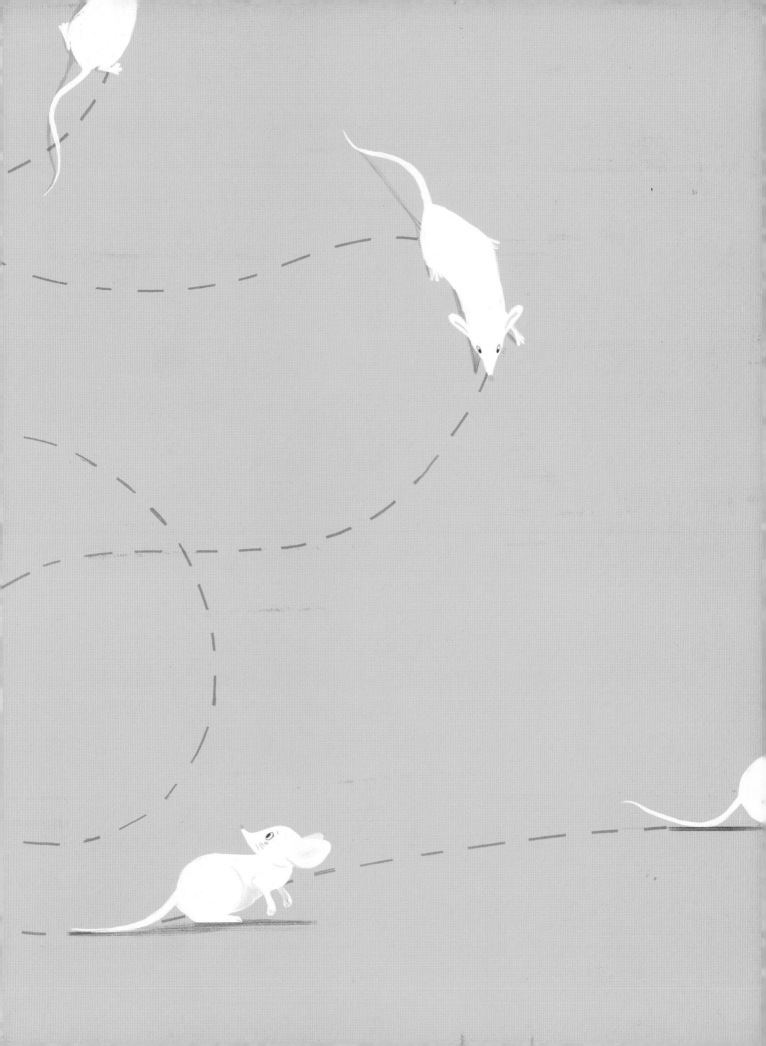

For my dad, Ned Nelkin, who always believed in me.
May his memory be a blessing.
—J.N.W.

Text copyright © 2020 by Joy Nelkin Wieder • Jacket art and interior illustrations copyright © 2020 by Shahar Kober • All rights reserved. Published in the United States by Doubleday, an imprint of Random House Children's Books, a division of Penguin Random House LLC, New York. • Doubleday and the colophon are registered trademarks of Penguin Random House LLC. • Visit us on the Web! rhcbooks.com • Educators and librarians, for a variety of teaching tools, visit us at RHTeachersLibrarians.com • Library of Congress Cataloging-in-Publication Data is available upon request. • ISBN 978-1-9848-9551-6 (trade) — ISBN 978-1-9848-9552-3 (lib. bdg.) — ISBN 978-1-9848-9553-0 (ebook) • MANUFACTURED IN CHINA • 10 9 8 7 6 5 4 3 2 1 • First Edition
Random House Children's Books supports the First Amendment and celebrates the right to read.

In a quiet village lived a lonely widow named Rivka. Every spring, she prepared her house for Passover.

All alone, she scrubbed and polished and swept her tiny cottage. Rivka had to remove all leavened food, or chometz—down to the last bread crumb!

All alone, she searched for any remaining crumbs the night before Passover. By the light of a candle, Rivka swept the final bits with a feather.

All alone, she piled the chometz on the table, to be burned in her fireplace the next morning.

At sunrise the next day, Rivka awoke and went to the kitchen to make a cup of tea. Suddenly a white mouse darted out of its hole.

Faster than Rivka could gasp, the mouse dashed up a table leg and climbed the mountain of chometz. At the tip-top, the mouse seized a piece of bread in its mouth. Then it jumped off the table, scattering crumbs everywhere. Rivka grabbed her broom. "Stop! Thief!"

The mouse ran into the street.

Rivka rushed out the door, screaming, "A mouse! A mouse! Took bread out of my house!"

Everyone in the village had just finished weeks of cleaning for Passover. Now the runaway mouse could ruin all their hard work. Bread was not allowed in anyone's home during Passover. And the holiday would start soon!

Menachem, the rabbi's youngest son, tried to catch the white mouse, but the little rodent scampered into the cobbler's house. Soon the cobbler and his wife rushed out the door, screaming, "A mouse! A mouse! Brought bread into our house!"

The cobbler shook his finger at Menachem and Rivka.
"Now we'll have to search for chometz yet again!"
Rivka's face turned red as borscht.

Suddenly a black mouse scurried out of the cobbler's house with a piece of bread in its mouth.

Did the black mouse take the bread away from the white mouse— or did it find another piece of bread in the cobbler's house? Maybe the cobbler and his wife hadn't found all their bread!

They all chased the black mouse, but it ran into the matchmaker's house.

Soon the matchmaker and her children rushed out the door,
screaming, "A mouse! A mouse! Brought bread into our house!"
They scowled at the cobbler, the cobbler's wife, Menachem,
and Rivka. "Now we'll have to search for chometz yet again!"

By this time, most of the village had come to see what was wrong. Just then, a cat leapt out of the matchmaker's house with a piece of bread in its mouth.

"Look!" shouted a yeshiva student. "The cat must have swallowed the mouse and taken the very same piece of bread that the rodent brought into the house."

"Then they won't have to search for chometz again," said Menachem.

"But what if the cat did not swallow the mouse? The bread could still be in the house!" cried the butcher.

A great argument arose. Some claimed the homes must be searched again; others said there was no need.

"Let's ask the rabbi," Rivka suggested.

The villagers knocked at the rabbi's door. "What's this all about?" asked the learned man.

Rivka explained what had happened.

"The Talmud will tell us what to do," said the rabbi.

After consulting the book of Jewish laws, the great man said, "According to the sages . . ."

The people pressed closer to hear him speak.

". . . this matter is undecided."

The crowd moaned.

"So, what are we to do?" asked Rivka.

The rabbi pulled on his beard. At last, he said, "To be absolutely sure, all the homes invaded by the creatures carrying chometz must be searched again."

"Oy vey!" the matchmaker wailed. "There's still much work to be done before Seder tonight."

Rivka said, "I must make the matzoh balls and chop the apples and nuts for the charoset. And I only have a short time left to burn the chometz! I'm all alone. How can I finish my work before sundown?"

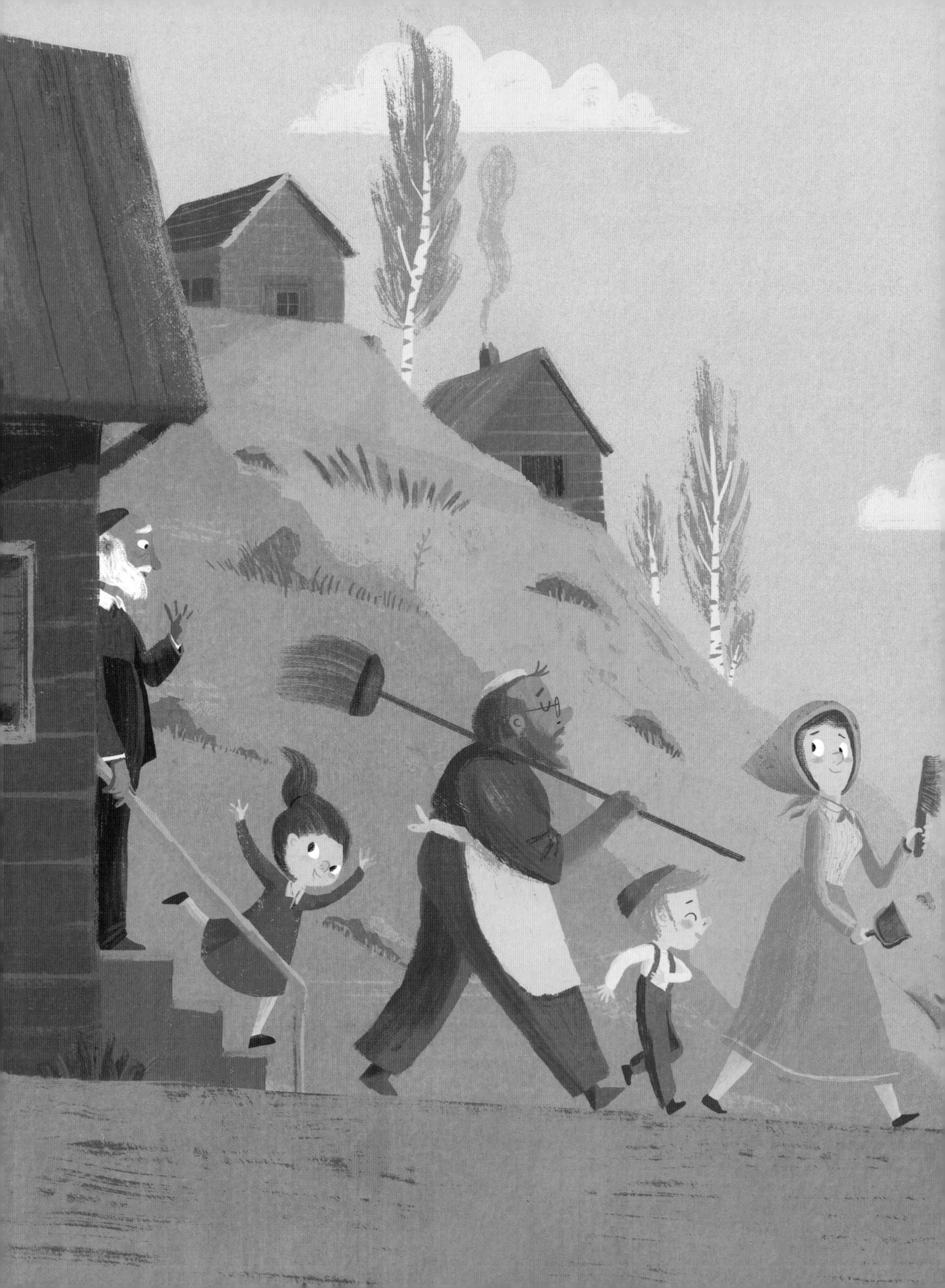

Menachem stepped forward. "I'll help you."

The cobbler and his wife said, "We need help, too."

"If everyone pitches in, then the work will be done in no time," said Menachem.

"A blessing on your head, my son." The rabbi turned to the villagers. "So, it is agreed?"

The people called out, "Yes, we'll help."

The rabbi assigned villagers to the homes in question.

All together, they searched Rivka's cottage, burned the chometz, and prepared the festive meal. Rivka was so pleased that she invited her helpers to stay for Seder.

When it came time for the Four Questions, Menachem proudly chanted, "*Mah nishtanah* . . . Why is this night different from all other nights?"

Rivka smiled. On all other nights, her home was empty, but on this night, it overflowed with friends.

After retelling the story of the Exodus, drinking the four cups of wine, and singing joyous songs of freedom, Rivka's visitors finally bade her good night.

But before she went to sleep, Rivka remembered one last guest.

"On this night, even a thief shouldn't go to bed hungry!"

AUTHOR'S NOTE

This original tale is based on a passage from the Talmud, a collection of ancient rabbis' commentaries on Jewish law. A section of the Talmud, Tractate Pesachim, discusses the laws and customs of Passover. It is forbidden to eat leavened food during all the days of the holiday, and chometz may not be owned or seen in one's home. Therefore, weeks of cleaning are followed by a final search with a candle and feather on the evening before Passover. The next day, the remaining chometz is burned before midday.

The Jewish sages discussed the possibility of mice bringing chometz into a house that had already been searched for it. They debated whether the home had to be searched again.

"Rava propounded a question: 'If a mouse entered a house and another came out of the same house and both had pieces of chometz in their mouths, shall we presume that it was the same mouse in both cases or not? . . . If the mouse entering was black and the other was white, shall we assume that one took the piece of bread away from the other or that there were two separate pieces of bread? . . . How would it be if a mouse entered with the piece of bread and a cat came out with a piece of bread? If we presume that the piece of bread is the same, would the cat not have held the mouse in its mouth also? If then you say that the piece of bread was a different piece, how would it be if the cat came out with the mouse and the piece of bread in its mouth?' . . . This question is not decided." (*The Babylonian Talmud*, Pesachim 10b, translated by Michael L. Rodkinson)

GLOSSARY

borscht (BORSHT)—a type of beet soup

charoset (kha-RO-set)—a ceremonial dish often made with apples and nuts, used for the Seder

chometz (KHA-mets)—leavened foods, not allowed during Passover, such as bread, cake, cookies, and crackers

Exodus (EX-uh-dus)—the escape of the Israelites, or Jews, from slavery in ancient Egypt, as told in the second book of the Bible

Four Questions—a section of the Seder sung by the youngest person at the table

leavened (LEH-vend) **foods**—bread and other foods that have been allowed to ferment and rise

matzoh (MA-tzah)—unleavened bread

Oy vey (OY VAY)—a Yiddish expression meaning "Oh, how terrible!"

Passover (PASS-oh-ver)—the festival celebrating the Exodus of the Jews from ancient Egypt

rabbi (RAB-eye)—a person ordained as a Jewish religious leader

sage (SAYJ)—an ancient teacher respected for great wisdom

Seder (SAY-der)—the ceremony and festive dinner celebrated at the start of Passover

Talmud (TALL-mud)—a collection of Jewish laws with commentaries by ancient rabbis

yeshiva (yuh-SHEE-vuh)—a school for the study of Jewish texts, like the Talmud